P9-DME-945

GLAD MONSTER SAD MONSTER

a book about feelings

by Ed Emberley & Anne Miranda

HOW TO USE THIS BOOK:

1. Open the monster flap.

2. Read the text.   3. Try on the mask.   Have fun pretending!

SCHOLASTIC INC.

New York Toronto London Auckland Sydney

The yellow monster says,
"Opening birthday presents,

playing ball,

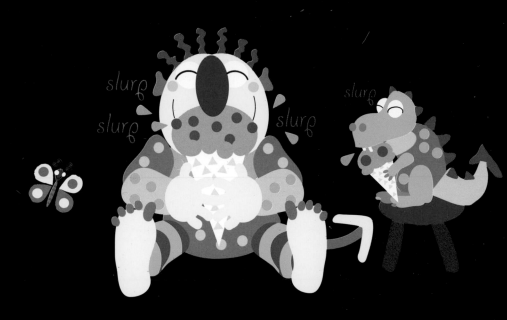

slurping ice cream,

and dancing with my friend
make me glad."

The blue monster says, "Waving good-bye,

watching my snowmonster melt,

Try on the yellow monster mask.
What makes you glad?

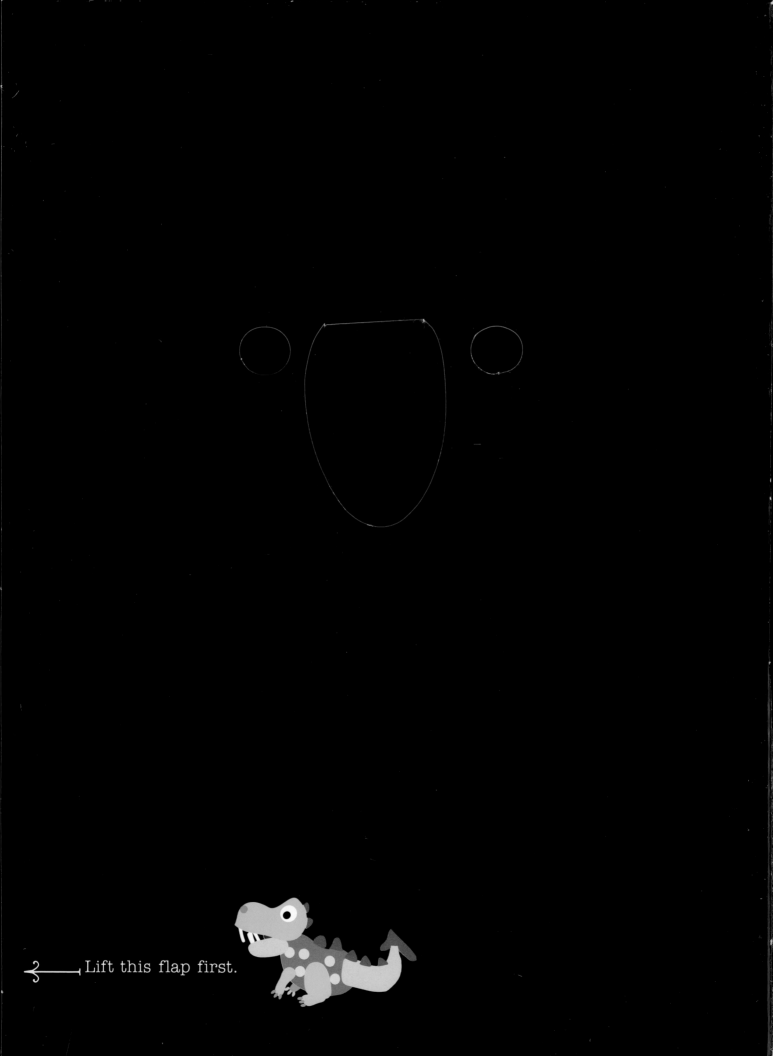

Lift this flap first.

Lift this flap first.

Pretend to be a sad blue monster.
Have you ever been sad, too?

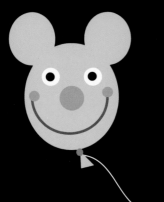

losing my big blue balloon,

and having it rain on parade day
make me sad."

The pink monster says, "Making Valentines,

rocking baby monster,

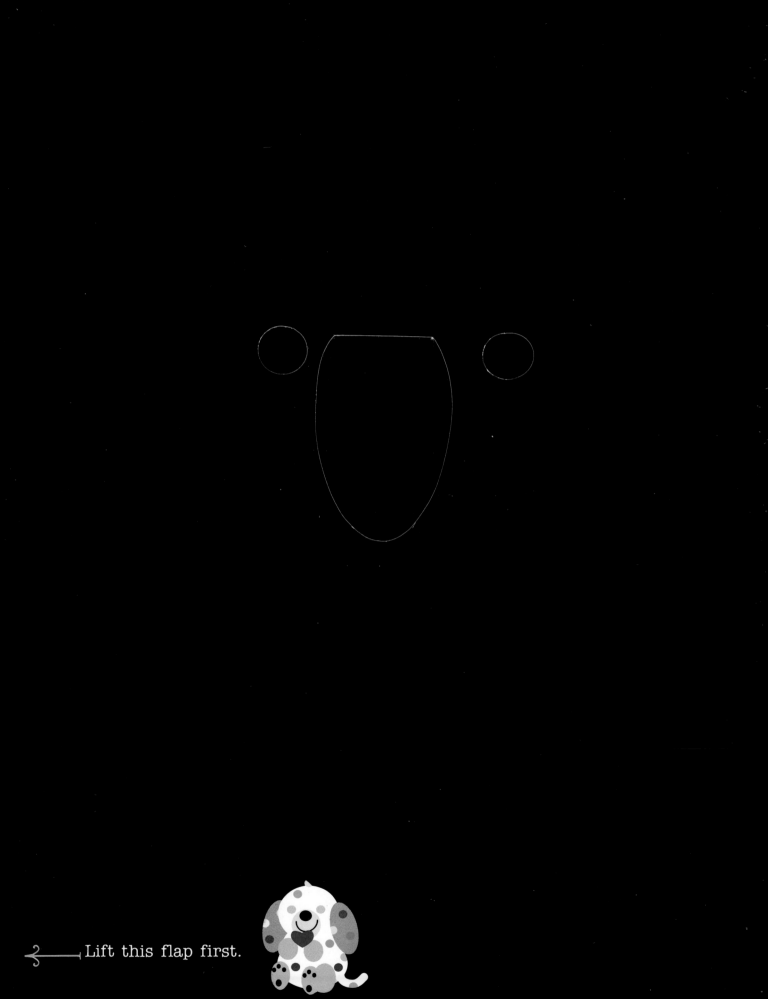

Lift this flap first.

Put on the pink monster mask.
Tell what makes you feel loving.

baking muffins with Grammy Monster,

and hugging wiggly puppies
make me feel loving."

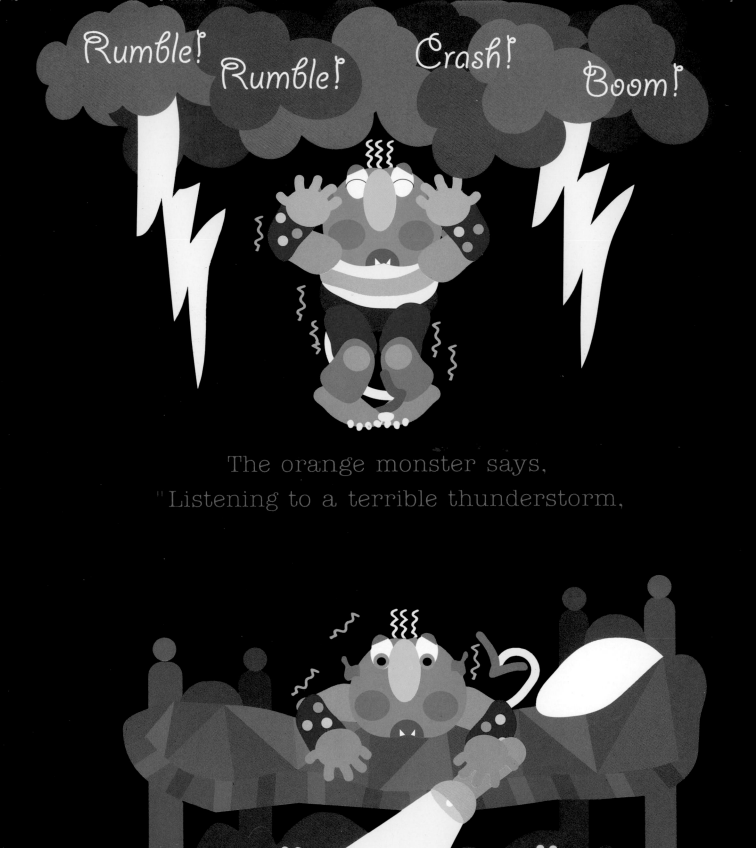

Rumble! Rumble! Crash! Boom!

The orange monster says,
"Listening to a terrible thunderstorm,

imagining what's hiding under my bed,

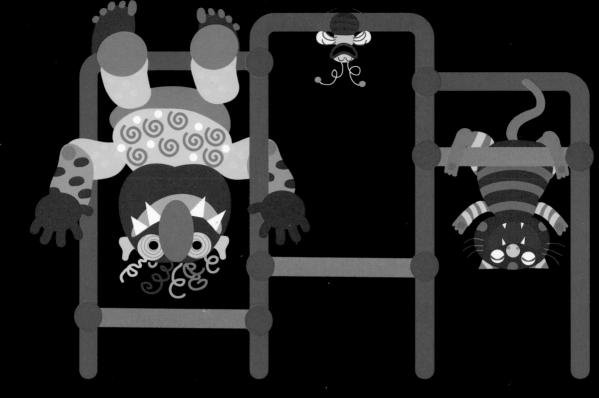

he purple monster says, "Being upside down,

Lahlah!

Lahlah!

seeing little creepy-crawly things,

and being chased by grumpy growly things
worry me. "

Can you act like the orange monster?
What worries you?

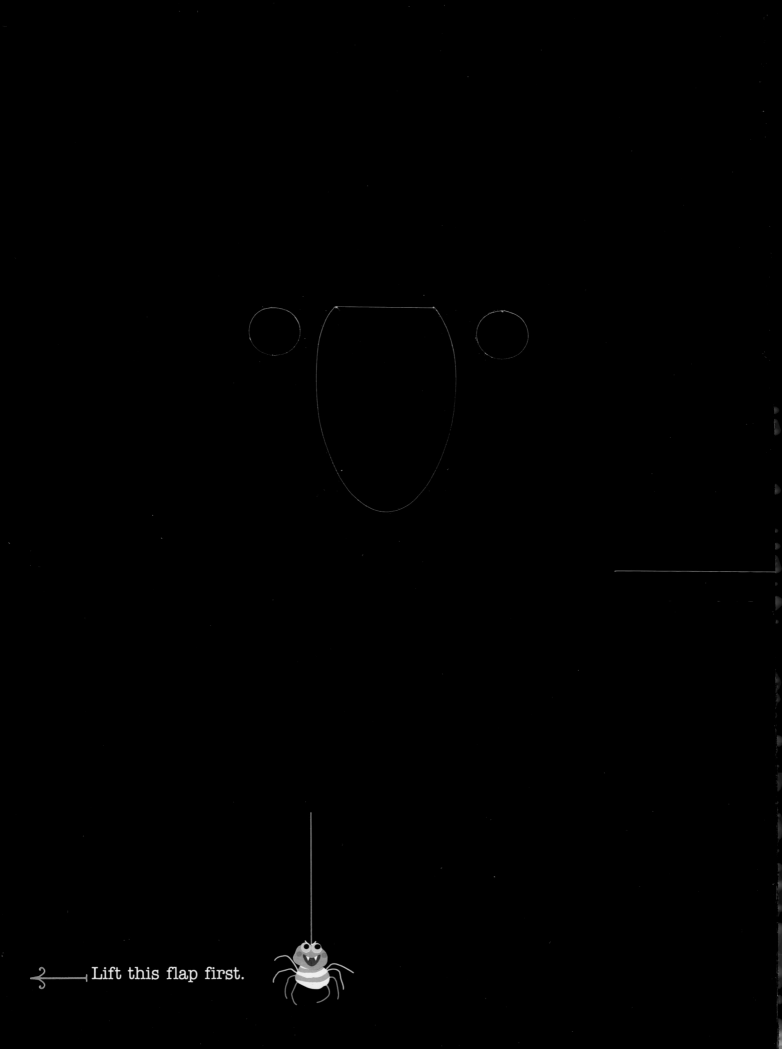

Lift this flap first.

The red monster says, "Being bugged by a bug,

getting splashed,

wearing Big Monster's clothes,

Goink!

Goink!

Goink!

and goinking around make me feel silly."

Pretend to be a purple monster.
How silly can you be?

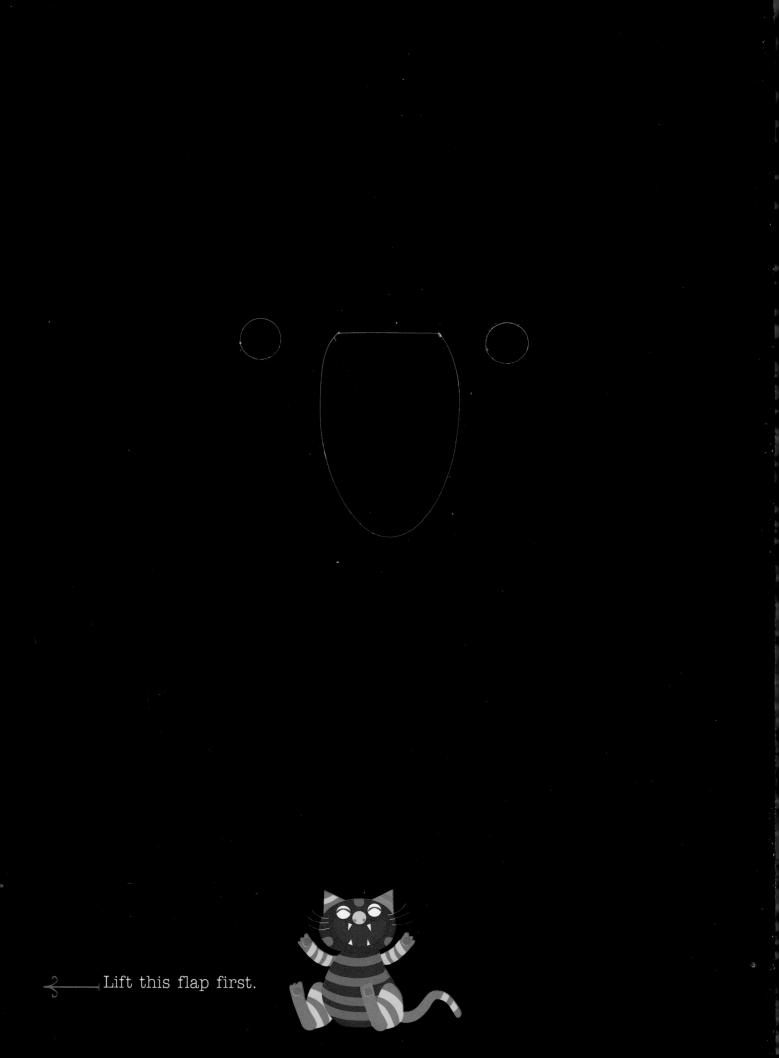

Lift this flap first.

The green monster says,
"Growling, showing my sharp white teeth,

waving my hands in the air,
and saying Shoo! Shoo!

being laughed at when I fall down,

and having someone knock over my blocks
make me angry."

Put on the angry red monster mask.
Say what makes you angry.

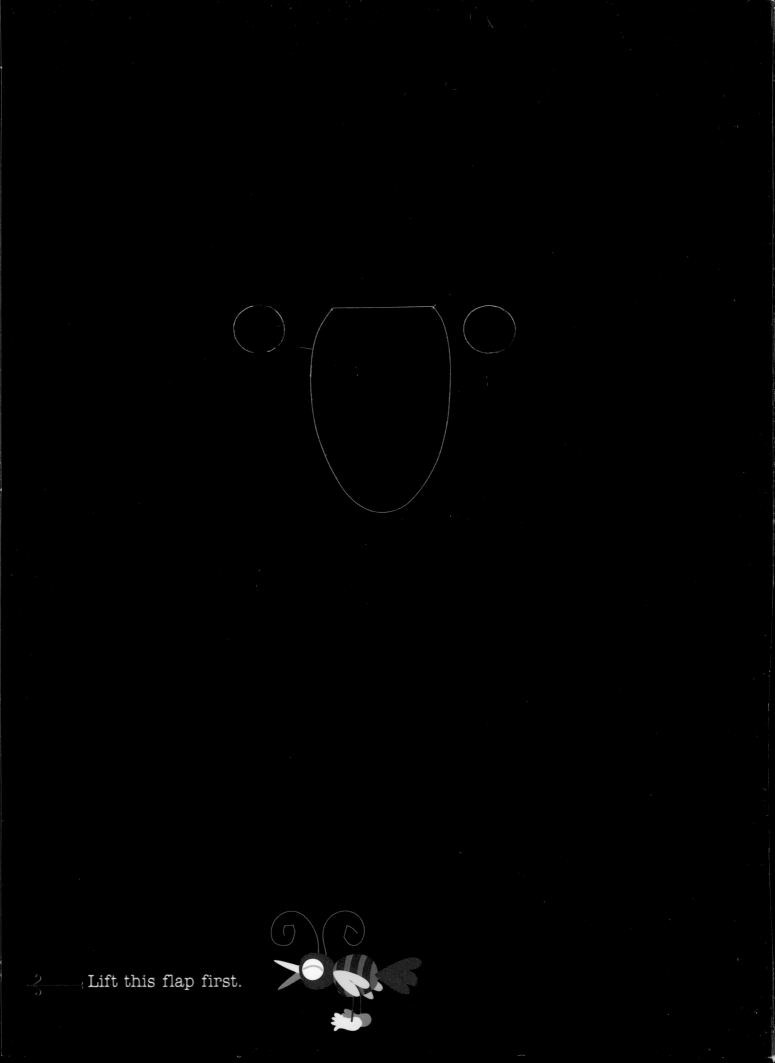

Lift this flap first.

Boo!

Boo!

Boo!

Boo!

Boo!

Boo!

Boo!

No part of this publication may be reproduced in whole or in part, or stored in a retrieval system, or transmitted in any form or by any means, electronic, mechanical, photocopying, recording, or otherwise, without written permission of the publisher. For information regarding permission, write to Little, Brown and Company (Inc.), 34 Beacon Street, Boston, MA 02108.

ISBN 0-590-03708-0

Text copyright © 1997 by Anne Miranda.
Illustrations copyright © 1997 by Ed Emberley.
All rights reserved. Published by Scholastic Inc., 555 Broadway, New York, NY 10012, by arrangement with Little, Brown and Company (Inc.).

SCHOLASTIC and associated logos are trademarks and/or registered trademarks of Scholastic Inc.

12 11 10 9   8 9 10 11/0

Printed in Thailand   53

First Scholastic printing, September 1998

Boo! Boo!

and Boo! Boo!
make me very scary!"

Put on this green monster mask.
Can you scare me? Can I scare you?

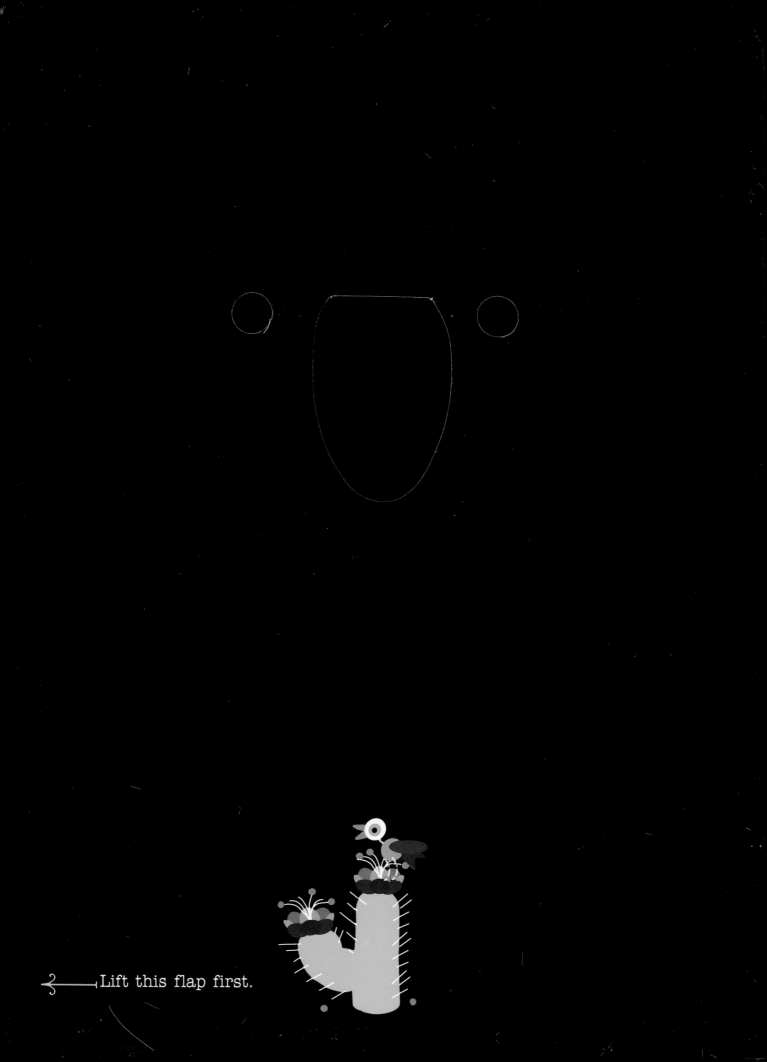

Lift this flap first.